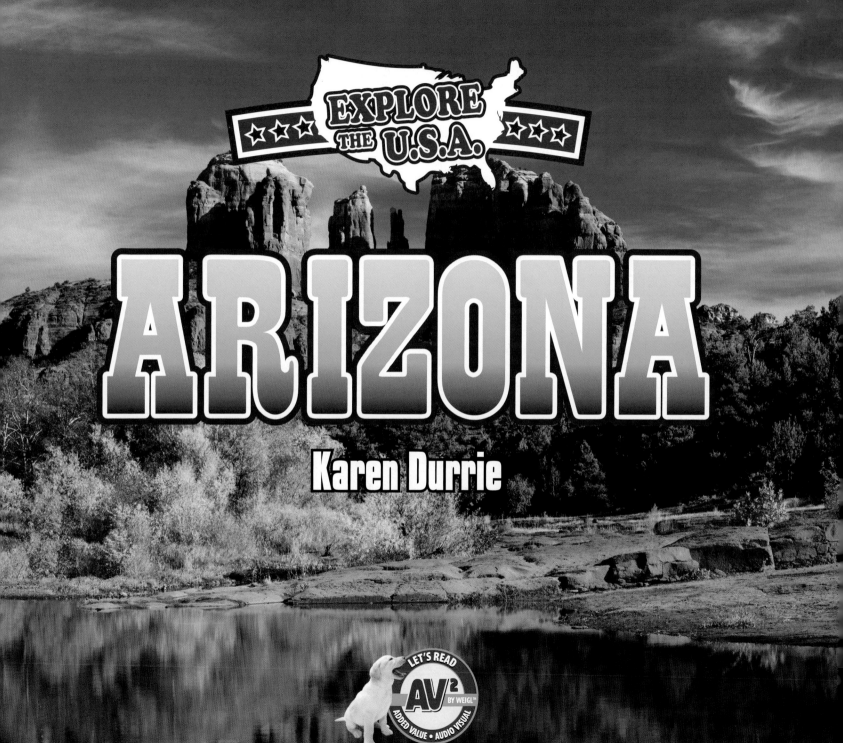

EXPLORE THE U.S.A.

ARIZONA

Karen Durrie

LET'S READ
AV²
BY WEIGL™
ADDED VALUE • AUDIO VISUAL

Go to www.av2books.com, and enter this book's unique code.

BOOK CODE

J177437

AV² by Weigl brings you media enhanced books that support active learning.

AV² provides enriched content that supplements and complements this book. Weigl's AV² books strive to create inspired learning and engage young minds in a total learning experience.

Your AV² Media Enhanced books come alive with...

Audio
Listen to sections of the book read aloud.

Video
Watch informative video clips.

Embedded Weblinks
Gain additional information for research.

Try This!
Complete activities and hands-on experiments.

Key Words
Study vocabulary, and complete a matching word activity.

Quizzes
Test your knowledge.

Slide Show
View images and captions, and prepare a presentation.

... and much, much more!

Published by AV² by Weigl
350 5th Avenue, 59th Floor
New York, NY 10118
Website: www.av2books.com   www.weigl.com

Library of Congress Cataloging-in-Publication Data

Durrie, Karen.
 Arizona / Karen Durrie.
   p. cm. -- (Explore the U.S.A.)
 Includes bibliographical references and index.
 ISBN 978-1-61913-325-9 (hard cover : alk. paper)
 1. Arizona--Juvenile literature. I. Title.
 F811.3.D87 2012
 979.1--dc23
                              2012014755

Printed in the United States of America in North Mankato, Minnesota
1 2 3 4 5 6 7 8 9   16 15 14 13 12

052012
WEP040512

Project Coordinator: Karen Durrie
Art Director: Terry Paulhus

Weigl acknowledges Getty Images as the primary image supplier for this title.

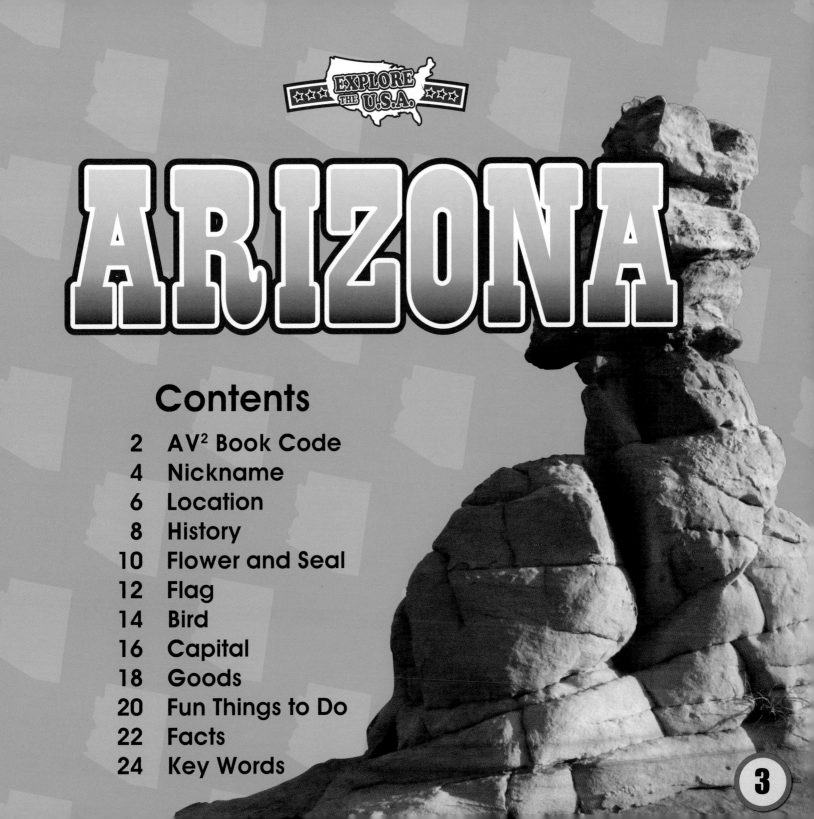

ARIZONA

Contents

EXPLORE THE U.S.A.

3

This is Arizona.
It is the Grand Canyon State.
The Grand Canyon is
277 miles long.

This is the shape of Arizona. It is in the south part of the United States.

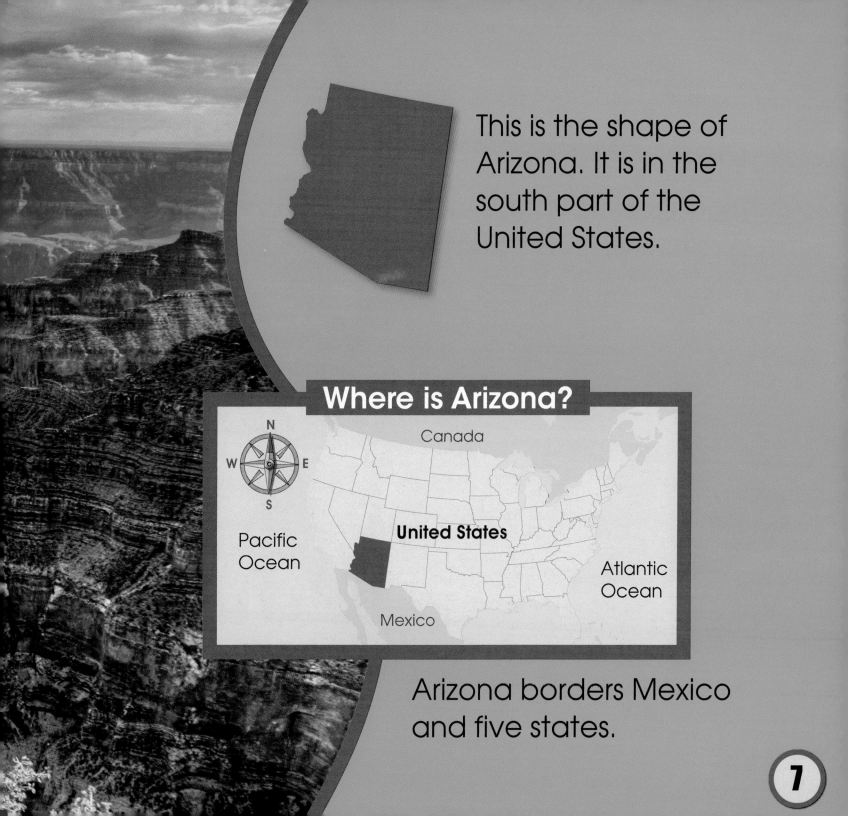

Where is Arizona?

Canada

United States

Pacific Ocean

Atlantic Ocean

Mexico

Arizona borders Mexico and five states.

Arizona has the oldest American Indian village in the United States. The village was built about 850 years ago.

People still live in the village today.

9

The white saguaro is the Arizona state flower. It blooms on a cactus in the summer.

The state seal has a man, the Sun, and a cow.

The man on the seal is a miner.

This is the state flag of Arizona. It has a copper star in the middle.

Red and yellow stand for the beautiful sunsets in Arizona.

The cactus wren is the Arizona state bird. Its nest is the size of a football. It makes its nest from grass and other plants.

The cactus wren builds its nest in a cactus.

15

This is the largest city in Arizona. It is named Phoenix. It is the state capital.

Phoenix has the largest city park on Earth.

Copper can be found in Arizona. People dig mines to get copper. Copper is used to make many things.

Pennies are made with copper.

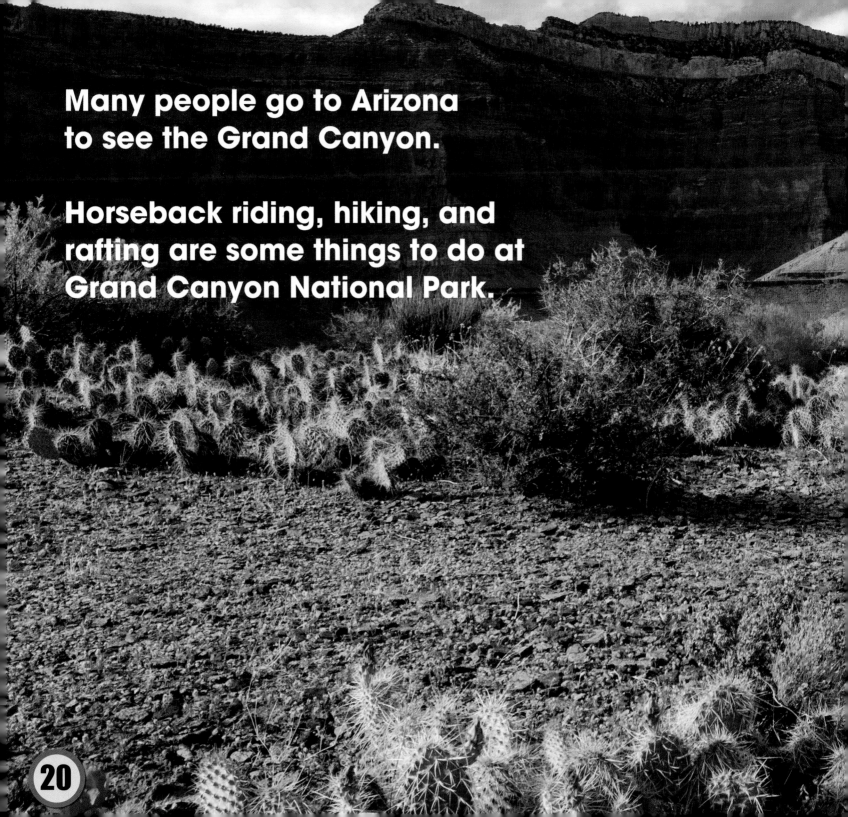

Many people go to Arizona to see the Grand Canyon.

Horseback riding, hiking, and rafting are some things to do at Grand Canyon National Park.

ARIZONA FACTS

These pages provide detailed information that expands on the interesting facts found in the book. These pages are intended to be used by adults as a learning support to help young readers round out their knowledge of each state in the *Explore the U.S.A.* series.

Pages 4–5

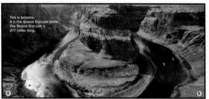

The Grand Canyon is a geographical feature that was created by water eroding rock and land. The Grand Canyon is 277 miles (446 kilometers) long and 18 miles (29 km) wide. Archaeologists have found human artifacts such as pots in the area. The pots are about 12,000 years old.

Pages 6–7

On February 14, 1912, Arizona became the 48th state to join the United States. It shares borders with five states. Arizona is known as a Four Corners state. Its northeastern corner borders Utah, New Mexico, and Colorado. The borders come together at precise angles to make four corners. Arizona also borders California and Nevada to the west.

Pages 8–9

The Hopi people built a settlement in present-day Arizona in 1100. In 1540, the settlement was discovered by Spanish explorer Pedro de Tovar. The village at Oraibi was one of the largest Hopi villages in 1900, with a population of more than 800. It is one of the oldest continually inhabited villages in the United States.

Pages 10–11

The saguaro cactus is the largest cactus that grows in the United States. These cacti grow between 40 and 60 feet (12 and 18 meters) tall. Most saguaro roots only grow 4 to 6 inches (10 to 15 centimeters) underground. Saguaro blossoms grow in May and June. The state seal of Arizona features the industries of the state, such as mining, agriculture, and ranching.

The state flag was designed in 1917. It features a copper star in the center. The color represents the importance of the copper industry to Arizona. There are 13 yellow and red Sun rays on the flag. These represent the original 13 colonies of the United States.

The cactus wren is a small bird. It can be up to 8 inches (20 cm) long. The cactus wren has white stripes over both eyes. It is known to build multiple nests as decoys to fool predators. The state mammal is the ringtail, which is related to the raccoon.

Phoenix became the state capital in 1912. The city is home to 1.4 million people, making it the fifth-largest city in the United States. South Mountain Park is the largest urban park in the world. It is a nature preserve covering more than 16,000 acres (6,475 hectares). People use the park to hike, ride horses, and mountain bike.

Arizona is the largest producer of copper in the United States. Copper mined from Arizona makes up 65 percent of the total copper production in the country. Copper and zinc are used to make pennies. Other minerals are mined in Arizona, including silver, perlite, sand, gravel, and gemstones such as quartz and turquoise.

The Grand Canyon is 18 miles (29 km) wide in some places, and up to 1 mile (1.6 km) deep. Five million people visit the Grand Canyon each year. Mule riding, river trips, camping, and guided educational tours are some of the activities people do when visiting the Grand Canyon.

KEY WORDS

Research has shown that as much as 65 percent of all written material published in English is made up of 300 words. These 300 words cannot be taught using pictures or learned by sounding them out. They must be recognized by sight. This book contains 50 common sight words to help young readers improve their reading fluency and comprehension. This book also teaches young readers several important content words, such as proper nouns. These words are paired with pictures to aid in learning and improve understanding.

Page	Sight Words First Appearance
4	is, it, long, miles, state, the, this
7	and, in, of, part, where
8	about, American, has, Indian, live, people, still, was, years
11	a, man, on, white
12	for
15	from, its, makes, other, plants
16	city, Earth, named
19	are, be, can, found, get, made, many, things, to, used, with
20	at, do, go, see, some

Page	Content Words First Appearance
4	Arizona, Grand Canyon
7	Mexico, shape, United States
8	village
11	cactus, cow, flower, miner, seal, summer, Sun, saguaro
12	flag, middle, star, sunsets
15	bird, cactus wren, football, grass, nest, size
16	capital, park, Phoenix
19	copper, mines, pennies
20	Grand Canyon National Park, horseback riding, hiking, rafting

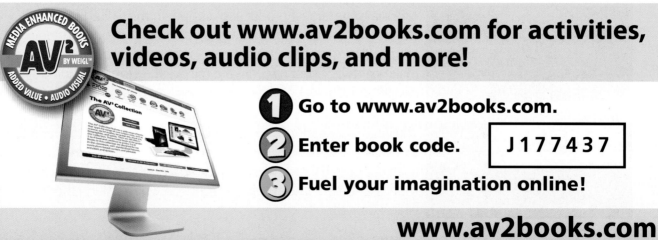